Dragon Feathers

Translated by Polly Lawson
First published in German as *Die Drachenfedern* 1993
This edition published in English by Floris Books 2010
© 1993 Esslinger Verlag J F Schreiber, Esslingen, Germany
This translation © 2010 Floris Books, Edinburgh

British Library CIP Data available
ISBN 978-086315-774-5
Printed in Belgium by Proost

Dragon Feathers

Illustrated by Andrei Dugin and Olga Dugina

Retold by Arnica Esterl

Floris Books

There was once a rich innkeeper who had a beautiful daughter called Beth. Next door to them lived a poor woodcutter and his son — the most handsome young man in the village. He was hardworking, cheerful and always willing to help his neighbours. But every time he saw Beth, his heart skipped a beat; he liked her so much.

Beth was very fond of the woodcutter's son, but because he was so poor her father would never agree to let them marry. But was there any harm in trying? So they did.

The innkeeper told his daughter not to be so silly. He laughed at the woodcutter's son. "If you want my daughter's hand in marriage, go to the dragon's castle in the dark forest, pluck three feathers from the dragon's back and bring them to me."

Although he knew how fierce the dragon was, the boy was convinced he could trick the terrible beast. And so he set off for the dragon's castle.

On his way, he came to a house where a man was sitting outside with his head in his hands.

"Why are you so sad?" asked the woodcutter's son.

"My daughter has been ill for many years, and only the dragon in the dark forest can help her. But who will ...?"

"Well, I'm on my way to see the dragon," the woodcutter's son interrupted. "I'll ask him for a remedy, and tell you when I return."

The boy went on, until he came to a clearing where a crowd of people were gathered around an apple tree.

"Is there something special about this tree?" asked the woodcutter's son.

"Oh yes, this is a very special tree," said one of the crowd. "It used to bear golden apples, but now it doesn't even have a leaf! The only creature who might know why is the dragon in the dark forest."

"I'm on my way to see the dragon, so I'll ask him," said the boy.

Soon the woodcutter's son could see the dark forest on the far side of a river, shrouded in mist. He hurried along to the riverbank, where a fisherman ferried him across.

"I've been doing this tedious job for so long now," the fisherman complained. "But there's no one else to do it. If only I had time to go and ask the dragon. He might give me good advice."

The woodcutter's son told him of his quest, and promised to ask the dragon's advice.

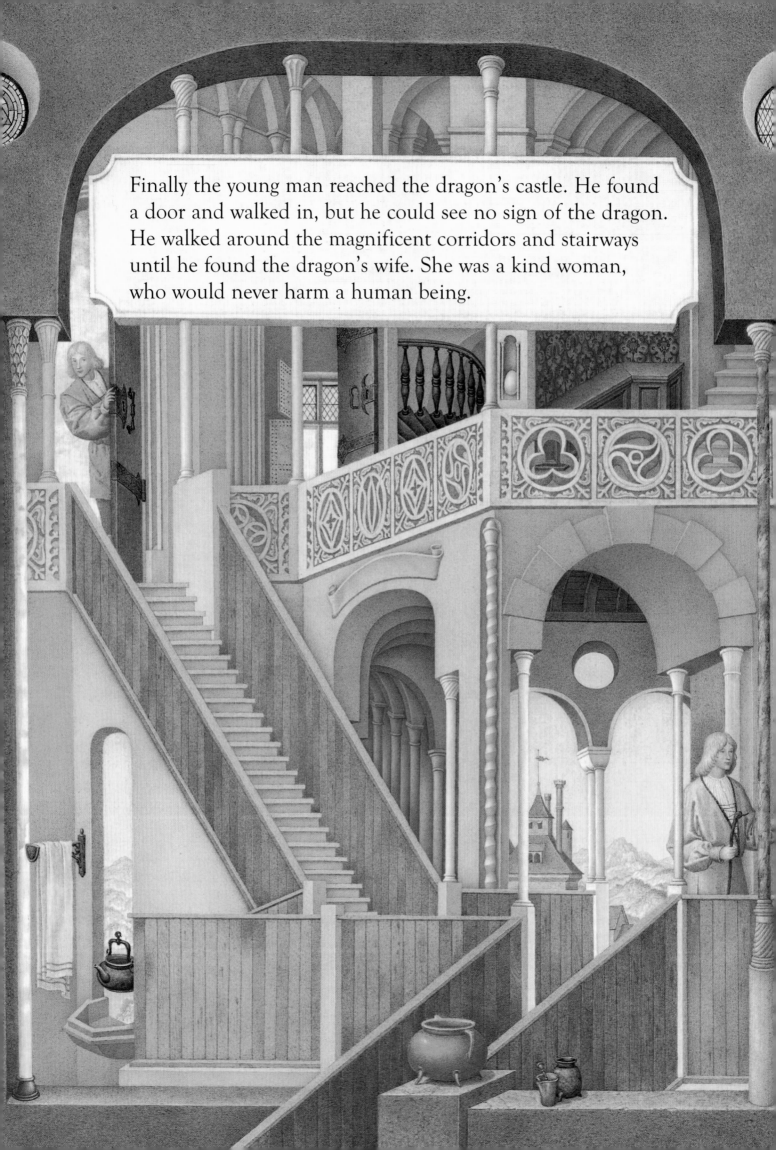

Finally the young man reached the dragon's castle. He found a door and walked in, but he could see no sign of the dragon. He walked around the magnificent corridors and stairways until he found the dragon's wife. She was a kind woman, who would never harm a human being.

She asked him what he wanted, and he told her that he
needed three feathers from the dragon's back; he told her
about the man whose daughter was ill, about the withered
apple tree and the fisherman.

The dragon's wife said, "No human can speak to the
dragon without being eaten. But if you hide under the bed
and listen, I will ask him about these things myself."

Late that night the dragon came home, even more fierce than usual. He called angrily, "I can taste ... I can smell a human!" "Oh no," his wife replied sweetly, "no one has been here." Eventually the dragon calmed down, soothed by the soft words and gentle touch of his wife.

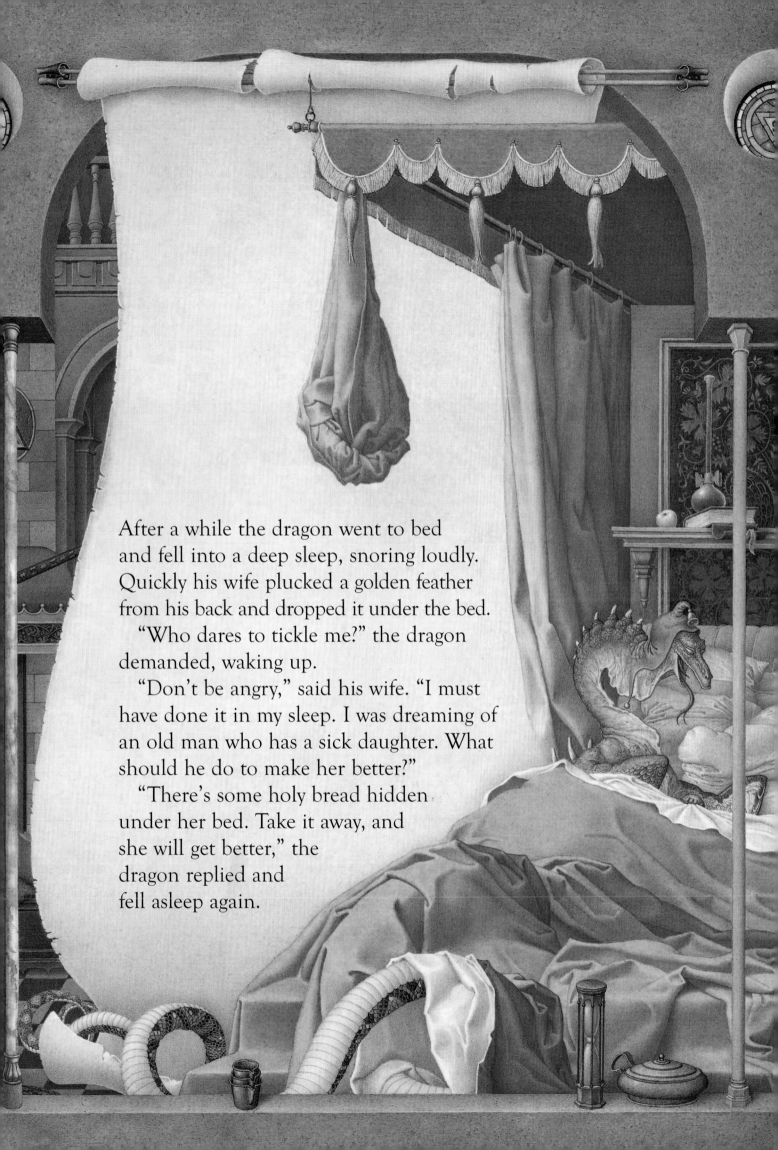

After a while the dragon went to bed
and fell into a deep sleep, snoring loudly.
Quickly his wife plucked a golden feather
from his back and dropped it under the bed.

"Who dares to tickle me?" the dragon
demanded, waking up.

"Don't be angry," said his wife. "I must
have done it in my sleep. I was dreaming of
an old man who has a sick daughter. What
should he do to make her better?"

"There's some holy bread hidden
under her bed. Take it away, and
she will get better," the
dragon replied and
fell asleep again.

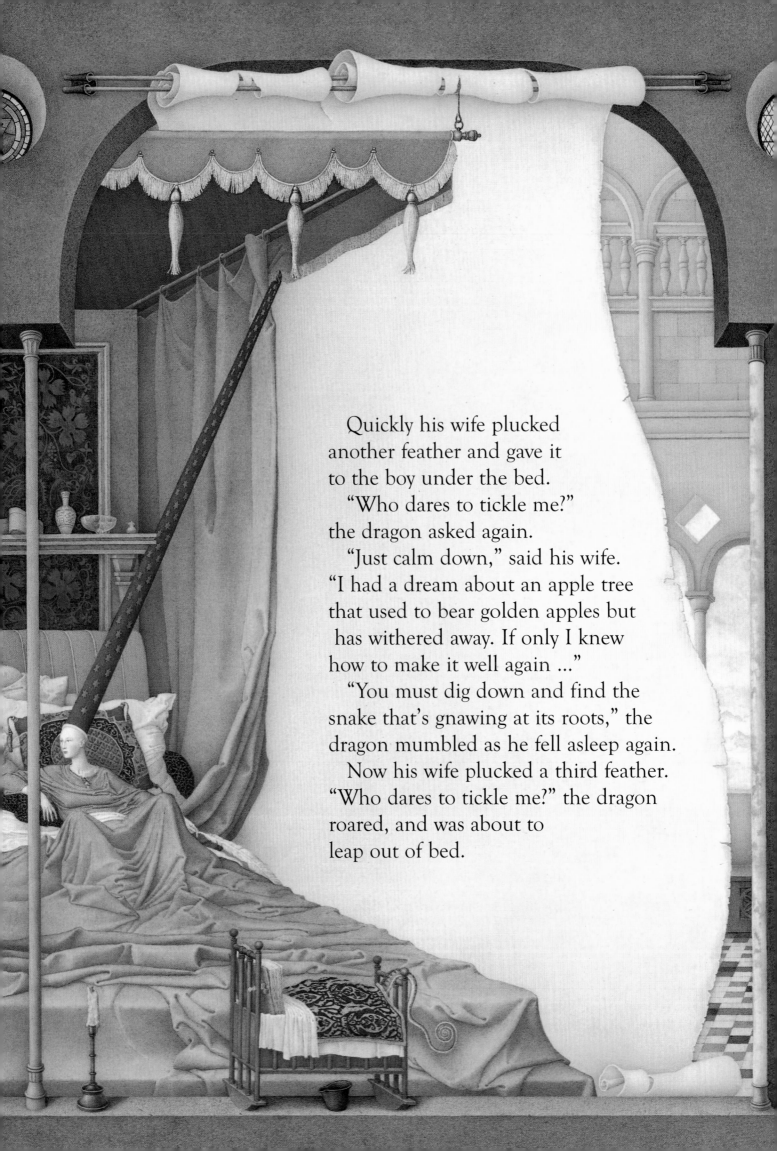

Quickly his wife plucked
another feather and gave it
to the boy under the bed.

"Who dares to tickle me?"
the dragon asked again.

"Just calm down," said his wife.
"I had a dream about an apple tree
that used to bear golden apples but
has withered away. If only I knew
how to make it well again ..."

"You must dig down and find the
snake that's gnawing at its roots," the
dragon mumbled as he fell asleep again.

Now his wife plucked a third feather.
"Who dares to tickle me?" the dragon
roared, and was about to
leap out of bed.

His wife held him back, saying, "Don't be angry. I was just dreaming of an old fisherman who has to ferry people over the river, and is never allowed to go free." "He should just give the oars to the first person he meets and run away, the silly old man," grumbled the dragon. "Now leave me in peace, or I shall tear you to pieces." The dragon fell asleep again, and the young man crept quietly out from under the bed and out of the castle.

At the river, the woodcutter's son met the fisherman,
who asked him about his meeting with the dragon.
"Ferry me over the river first," replied the boy.

When he got out of the boat, the woodcutter's son passed on the dragon's advice. "Give the oars to the next person who comes along," he said, but he didn't call him a silly old man.

The fisherman was overjoyed and gave the boy money and food.

The young man walked on until he reached the crowd of people who were still gathered around the apple tree. Together they dug at the roots and found the snake, and immediately leaves appeared and the tree grew golden apples. The people were so happy, they gave the boy gold and silver.

Next the woodcutter's son arrived at the house of the old man whose daughter was ill. He led him to his daughter's bed and found the hidden holy bread.
"Take the bread away," said the boy, "and your daughter will get better."
The father and daughter were so grateful that they gave the boy a bag of coins.

But the happiest of all was Beth, when the young man finally returned
home. She led him to her father, who gave his blessing for them to be
married; his poor neighbour's son was now even richer than him.
"Where in the world did you get those riches from?" the innkeeper asked.
"From the dragon in the dark forest," the boy replied.
"There's gold and silver lying around in heaps over there!"
And you can probably guess what the greedy innkeeper did next ...
He rushed off towards the dark forest, to be ferried across the river.
The young bride and groom invited all the villagers to a great feast.
There was dancing and merriment, and everyone was delighted that the
young man had returned home safe from his great adventure.
But no one was happier than the woodcutter's son
and his beautiful wife.